SNOOPY™
TO THE RESCUE

A PEANUTS™ Collection

CHARLES M. SCHULZ

Andrews McMeel
PUBLISHING®

Other *Peanuts* Kids' Collections

6

PSYCHIATRIC HELP 5¢

THE DOCTOR IS IN

I FIND MYSELF ALWAYS WORRYING ABOUT TOMORROW..

THEN WHEN TOMORROW BECOMES TODAY, I START WORRYING ABOUT TOMORROW AGAIN..

I GUESS I'M JUST AFRAID TO FACE THE FUTURE

I THINK I CAN HELP YOU, CHARLIE BROWN...

HELP 5¢

THE DOCTOR IS IN

NOW, THE FIRST THING YOU HAVE TO DO IS TURN AROUND...

THE FUTURE IS OVER THIS WAY... THERE, THAT'S BETTER!

!

NOW, THE NEXT THING IS YOUR POSTURE... IF YOU'RE GOING TO FACE THE FUTURE, YOU'VE GOT TO DO IT WITH YOUR CHEST OUT..

THAT'S THE WAY! THROW OUT YOUR CHEST AND FACE THE FUTURE! NOW, RAISE YOUR ARM AND CLENCH YOUR FIST..THAT'S RIGHT.. NOW, LOOK DETERMINED...

WELL, I THINK I KNOW WHY YOU'RE AFRAID TO FACE THE FUTURE..

WHY?

YOU LOOK RIDICULOUS!

SCHULZ

11

BOOT!

WHAT HAPPENED TO MY FOOTBALL? IT WAS HERE IN THE YARD A MINUTE AGO, BUT NOW IT'S GONE...

THE MAD PUNTER HAS STRUCK AGAIN

THUMB À LA MODE!

I'M WORKING ON OUR BASEBALL SCHEDULE FOR NEXT SEASON

GET US SOME GAMES WITH SOME REAL LITTLE KIDS, CHARLIE BROWN, SO WE CAN SLAUGHTER THEM...

AND THEN GET US SOME GAMES WITH SOME REAL OLD LADIES, AND WE'LL SLAUGHTER THEM, TOO!

PLAN OUR SCHEDULE RIGHT, CHARLIE BROWN, AND WE'LL HAVE A GREAT SEASON!

THAT'S THE LAST STRAW! IF HE WANTS ANY SUPPER, HE CAN COME AND GET IT HIMSELF!

SERVANTS' ENTRANCE IN THE REAR

SO HERE I AM ABOUT TO SEE THE SCHOOL NURSE..

SHE'LL PROBABLY JUST TAKE MY TEMPERATURE AND LOOK AT MY THROAT...

MAYBE SHE'LL TAKE A BLOOD TEST... I HOPE SHE DOESN'T TAKE A BLOOD TEST... MAYBE SHE'LL JUST WEIGH ME...

IF SHE MENTIONS EXPLORATORY SURGERY, I'LL SCREAM!

THE SCHOOL NURSE TOLD ME TO GO HOME UNTIL MY STOMACH FELT BETTER

I WISH IT WOULDN'T HURT ALL THE TIME...

OTHER PEOPLE'S STOMACHS DON'T HURT ALL THE TIME...

MAYBE I HAVE A CHEAP STOMACH!

PSYCHIATRIC HELP 5¢

THE DOCTOR IS IN

I HAD TO GO TO THE SCHOOL NURSE YESTERDAY BECAUSE MY STOMACH HURT...

YOU WORRY TOO MUCH, CHARLIE BROWN...NO WONDER YOUR STOMACH HURTS...YOU'VE GOT TO STOP ALL THIS SILLY WORRYING!

HOW DO I STOP?

THE DOCTOR IS IN

THAT'S **YOUR** WORRY! FIVE CENTS, PLEASE!!

THE DOCTOR IS IN

↓

WE WRIST WRESTLERS SHOW OUR OPPONENTS NO MERCY!

KLUNK!!

THIS IS VERY INTERESTING...

DID YOU KNOW THAT WRIST WRESTLERS HAVE THEIR OWN MOTTO?

"RAW STRENGTH AND COURAGE"

HOW FITTING!

LUCY, TASTE THIS THUMB FOR ME, WILL YOU, AND TELL ME IF YOU NOTICE ANYTHING PECULIAR ABOUT IT...

ARE YOU OUT OF YOUR MIND? GET YOUR STUPID THUMB AWAY FROM ME

"TASTE HIS THUMB"! GOOD GRIEF!

BLEAH!

I WAS RIGHT..

MENTHOL!!

35

DON'T BUG ME, DOG!

* SIGH *

SNOOPY HAS BEEN CHOSEN "ROOKIE OF THE YEAR"!

LOOK AT THE TROPHY THEY GAVE HIM!

AND THE BRONZE PLAQUE!

CONGRATULATIONS, SNOOPY! YOU DESERVED IT!

WOW! ONE OF MY OWN PLAYERS..ROOKIE OF THE YEAR! ISN'T THAT SOMETHING?

OKAY, TEAM! THAT PROVES WE'RE NOT SO BAD AFTER ALL! LET'S GET OUT THERE NOW AND WIN THIS GAME ...LET'S SHOW 'EM HOW TO PLAY!

BONK!

I KNOW WHAT AWARD I'LL WIN.."STOMACH-ACHE OF THE YEAR"!

I DON'T UNDERSTAND IT...

EVERY TIME SNOOPY GETS A LETTER FROM LILA, HE BECOMES VERY UPSET.. I DON'T EVEN KNOW WHAT LILA LOOKS LIKE..ONE TIME SHE CAME TO SEE HIM, AND HE RAN AND HID...

AND NOW WHAT HAPPENS? SHE WRITES TO HIM AGAIN, AND HE SUDDENLY TAKES OFF TO SEE HER! WHY? I DON'T UNDERSTAND IT!

LILA NEEDS ME!

WOW! WHAT A BIG HOSPITAL!

IF ANY OF THE NURSES CATCH ME, THEY'LL KILL ME... THEY HATE BEAGLES IN HOSPITALS...

LILA?

SNOOPY!!

HI, SWEETIE!

THE FIRST THING I DID IN MY INVESTIGATION, CHARLIE BROWN, WAS TO CALL THE DAISY HILL PUPPY FARM..

I FOUND OUT SOMETHING THAT WILL AMAZE YOU... IN FACT, I HESITATE TO TELL YOU....ARE YOU READY FOR A SHOCK?

KLUNK!

HE WASN'T READY FOR A SHOCK

WHAT HAPPENED?

HOW CAN I TELL YOU SOMETHING THAT WILL SHOCK YOU IF YOU PASS OUT BEFORE I CAN TELL YOU?

I'M SORRY... I'VE BEEN HYPERVENTILATING A LOT LATELY...

WELL, ANYWAY, HERE'S WHAT I FOUND OUT WHEN I CALLED THE DAISY HILL PUPPY FARM....YOU ARE **NOT** SNOOPY'S ORIGINAL OWNER!

KLUNK!

OH, GOOD GRIEF!

YOU BOUGHT SNOOPY IN THE MONTH OF OCTOBER, RIGHT?

ACCORDING TO THE RECORDS AT THE DAISY HILL PUPPY FARM, SNOOPY WAS BOUGHT BY ANOTHER FAMILY IN AUGUST...THIS FAMILY HAD A LITTLE GIRL NAMED LILA...

SNOOPY AND LILA LOVED EACH OTHER VERY MUCH, BUT THEY LIVED IN AN APARTMENT, AND THE FAMILY DECIDED THEY JUST COULDN'T KEEP SNOOPY SO THEY RETURNED HIM...

YOU GOT A USED DOG, CHARLIE BROWN!

NOW, I SEE WHY THOSE LETTERS FROM LILA WOULD UPSET SNOOPY SO MUCH

SURE, HE WAS TRYING TO FORGET HER, BUT WHEN HE FOUND OUT SHE WAS IN THE HOSPITAL, HE RAN OFF TO SEE HER...

I'LL BET HE WISHES HE WAS STILL HER DOG INSTEAD OF MINE...

I DOUBT IT, CHARLIE BROWN.. HE WOULDN'T HAVE BEEN HAPPY IN AN APARTMENT

HERE'S THE WORLD WAR I FLYING ACE ZOOMING THROUGH THE AIR IN HIS SOPWITH CAMEL!

WHEN I'M REAL LONESOME, I LIKE TO GO TO MY DAD'S BARBER SHOP..

HE ALWAYS SMILES WHEN I GO IN, AND SAYS, "HI"

THE TWO MEN WHO WORK WITH HIM ARE NICE TO ME, TOO..

THEY ALWAYS ASK ME IF I'VE COME IN FOR A SHAVE..

YOU LOOK WORRIED...

I AM WORRIED! WE'RE HAVING A TEST IN SCHOOL TOMORROW, AND THERE'S NO WAY I CAN PASS IT... ABSOLUTELY NO WAY!

HAVE YOU TRIED STUDYING?

WE'RE HAVING A TEST IN SCHOOL TOMORROW, AND THERE'S NO WAY I CAN PASS IT...ABSOLUTELY NO WAY!

I JUST LOST ANOTHER ARGUMENT WITH MY SISTER..

THAT'S BECAUSE YOU ALWAYS LET HER GET AWAY WITH USING MEANINGLESS GENERALITIES

THE NEXT TIME YOU ARGUE WITH HER, MAKE HER DEFINE HER TERMS...

THAT'S A GOOD IDEA

EATING ICE CREAM AGAIN, I SEE... YOU'RE GOING TO GET FAT!

FAT? I'M NOT FAT!

OF COURSE, YOU'RE FAT... LOOK AT THAT STOMACH!

DEFINE "STOMACH"!

I WONDER IF HE'S AUDITING THIS COURSE, OR TAKING IT FOR CREDIT...

YES, MA'AM?

YES, I KNOW HE ISN'T... YES, I'LL TELL HIM...

I'M SORRY, SNOOPY... YOU'LL HAVE TO GO HOME... DOGS AREN'T ALLOWED IN SCHOOL..

RATS! NOW, I'LL NEVER GET MY MASTER'S!

HE'S JUST THE TYPE WHO'LL MAKE CLASS PRESIDENT!

YES, MISS OTHMAR? THE STUDENT IN FRONT OF ME?

YES, MA'AM...I KNOW WHERE HE LIVES..I'LL TAKE HIM HOME..

I'M SORRY, SNOOPY.. I DON'T BLAME YOU FOR BEING OFFENDED..

SHE SHOULDN'T HAVE REFERRED TO YOU AS "THE FUNNY-LOOKING KID WITH THE BIG NOSE"

HELLO, CHUCK? THIS IS PEPPERMINT PATTY...

I'M MAKING OUT MY CHRISTMAS CARD LIST, CHUCK, AND I WANTED TO KNOW YOUR ADDRESS SO I COULD SURPRISE YOU WITH A CARD...

BUT NOW THE SURPRISE IS GONE, ISN'T IT? WELL, I'LL JUST SEND YOUR CARD TO SOMEONE ELSE SO I GUESS I WON'T NEED YOUR ADDRESS..FORGET I CALLED, CHUCK

SIGH

NUMBERS ARE BEAUTIFUL..

I LIKE TWOS THE BEST...THEY'RE SORT OF GENTLE..THREES AND FIVES ARE MEAN, BUT A FOUR IS ALWAYS PLEASANT.. I LIKE SEVENS AND EIGHTS, TOO, BUT NINES ALWAYS SCARE ME...TENS ARE GREAT...

HAVE YOU DONE THOSE DIVISION PROBLEMS FOR TOMORROW?

NOTHING SPOILS NUMBERS FASTER THAN A LOT OF ARITHMETIC!

IS IT CHRISTMAS YET?

FOUR MORE DAYS

HOW COME IT TAKES SO LONG?

CHRISTMAS IS ON TOP OF A STEEP HILL, AND THE CLOSER YOU GET TO IT, THE STEEPER THE HILL IS!

CHRISTMAS IS ON TOP OF A STEEP HILL!

ICE SKATING IS A GOOD WAY TO MEET GIRLS!

WELL, HOW IS YOUR YEAR COMING?

IT'S NOT MY YEAR ANY MORE.. I TOOK IT BACK...

THE MONTHS AND WEEKS WERE PRETTY GOOD, BUT IT HAD A LOT OF BAD DAYS IN IT...

THEY WERE VERY NICE ABOUT TAKING IT BACK..THEY SAID THIS HAPPENS ALL THE TIME

STUPID KID! I JUST HAD THAT CARPET IN THE FRONT HALL CLEANED!

CLOSE YOUR EYES, AND OPEN YOUR HANDS..

YOU DON'T TRUST ME, DO YOU? YOU LOOK LIKE YOU THINK I'M GOING TO PUT A WORM OR SOMETHING IN YOUR HANDS!

ALL RIGHT, JUST FOR THAT, I'M NOT GOING TO GIVE YOU WHAT I WAS GOING TO GIVE YOU!

I KNOW HER! SHE WANTS ME TO APOLOGIZE, AND THEN WHEN I CLOSE MY EYES AGAIN, SHE REALLY WILL DROP A WORM IN MY HANDS

I KNOW HIM.. HE THINKS I WANT HIM TO APOLOGIZE SO THAT I REALLY CAN DROP A WORM OR SOMETHING IN HIS HANDS...

I KNOW WHAT YOU'RE THINKING!

THIS IS RIDICULOUS.. HERE...TAKE THEM!

"THEM"?!!!

STUPID KITE!

THESE NIGHTS KILL ME..

EVERYTHING SEEMS SO HOPELESS AT NIGHT..

WHAT AM I DOING HERE? WHAT'S THE PURPOSE OF IT ALL?

WHAT'S GOING TO HAPPEN TO ME WHEN I GET OLD? WHAT IF I GET SICK? I DON'T WANT TO GET SICK..

WHAT IF I GET HIT BY A CAR SOMEDAY AND END UP IN A BODY CAST? OR MAYBE THEY'D JUST SHOOT ME LIKE AN OLD FARM HORSE! WHAT IF I LOST MY SIGHT OR MY HEARING?

Z

IT MUST BE NICE TO BE A DOG... THEY DON'T EVER HAVE ANY WORRIES...

NOT AS LONG AS THE SUN IS UP...

SCHULZ

SOME BUGS NEVER SMILE..

BUT YOU DON'T HAVE ANY IDEA WHERE SHE IS!

HOW WILL YOU FIND HER? WHERE WILL YOU LOOK? DON'T YOU THINK YOU SHOULD CONSIDER THIS A LITTLE MORE CAREFULLY BEFORE YOU JUST SORT OF TAKE OFF?

NO, YOUR MIND IS MADE UP, ISN'T IT? WELL, I HATE TO SEE YOU GO, BUT GOOD LUCK, OL' PAL... I HOPE YOU FIND HER...

MOM!

HE **WHAT?**

SNOOPY LEFT TO TRY TO FIND HIS MOTHER..

HE HASN'T HEARD FROM HER FOR A LONG TIME SO HE THOUGHT HE'D TRY TO FIND HER...

THAT STUPID BEAGLE! HE COULDN'T FIND ANYTHING!

MOM?

IT JUST KILLS ME WHEN SNOOPY GOES OFF ON THESE TRIPS..

HE HAS NO RIGHT TO WORRY YOU LIKE THIS, CHARLIE BROWN! HE'S YOUR DOG, AND HE SHOULD STAY HOME WHERE HE BELONGS!

BUT HE WANTS TO FIND HIS MOTHER..

THAT STUPID BEAGLE SHOULDN'T BE OUT ALONE! HE'LL BUMP INTO A TREE OR SOMETHING...

BONK!!

MOM?

IT'S RAINING, AND I'M LOST AND I CAN'T FIND MY MOM... I SHOULD HAVE STAYED HOME....

IF I WERE HOME, MY MASTER WOULD BE BRINGING ME MY SUPPER ABOUT NOW... WHAT WAS HIS NAME?

..THAT KID WITH THE ROUND HEAD..

IF SNOOPY'S BEEN GONE FOR FIVE DAYS, CHARLIE BROWN, I THINK YOU SHOULD PUT AN AD IN THE PAPER...

BUT WE DON'T KNOW IF HE'S LOST...

WELL, MAYBE HE'S IN TROUBLE...

IT'S DANGEROUS WANDERING AROUND THE COUNTRY..LOTS OF PECULIAR THINGS CAN HAPPEN...

GO 'WAY, YOU STUPID CAT!!

I **KNEW** I HEARD WINGS!

BEEP!

IT'S BEEN THREE HUNDRED AND EIGHTY-FOUR DAYS SINCE I LAST BEEPED YOU

THOSE WERE THREE HUNDRED AND EIGHTY-FOUR GOOD DAYS!

UNDERNEATH THE SOUND OF WALKING FEET AND SQUEAKING WHEELS I HEARD A COOKIE CRUNCH!

THIS IS MY "FIRST DAY OF MAY" DANCE

IT DIFFERS ONLY SLIGHTLY FROM MY "FIRST DAY OF FALL" DANCE, WHICH DIFFERS ALSO ONLY SLIGHTLY FROM MY "FIRST DAY OF SPRING" DANCE...

ACTUALLY, EVEN I HAVE A HARD TIME TELLING THEM APART...

↓

157

"TO CROSS STREET PUSH BUTTON..WAIT FOR WALK SIGNAL"

YOU HAVE TO MOVE YOUR FEET, TOO!

HOW EMBARRASSING!

ON A WARM SUNNY DAY LIKE TODAY, IN A NEIGHBORHOOD SUCH AS OURS, IT IS NOT OFTEN THAT YOU'LL SEE A BEAGLE FLOATING DOWNSTREAM!

THIS IS SATURDAY.. REAL VULTURES DON'T PERCH IN TREES ON SATURDAY

I DIDN'T KNOW THAT..

GRAMMA SAYS THAT NONE OF HER OTHER GRANDCHILDREN HAS A BLANKET

TELL GRAMMA THAT I'M VERY HAPPY FOR HER, AND THAT MY ADMIRATION FOR THOSE OTHER WONDERFULLY WELL-ADJUSTED GRANDCHILDREN KNOWS NO BOUNDS!

I DON'T THINK I'LL TELL HER THAT..

SNOOPY GOES ON THE ROAD AND FLIES TO THE MOON!

Snoopy is always up for fun times and great adventures. Discover the behind-the-scenes facts about the exciting journeys Snoopy had in this collection.

Thanks to our friends at the Charles M. Schulz Museum and Research Center in Santa Rosa, California, for letting us share their fascinating NASA information and photos.

To the Moon: Snoopy Soars in the Comics and with NASA

Snoopy was "the first beagle on the moon" earlier in this book, actually touching down on the lunar surface in March 1969, besting NASA's record by several months! In addition, Snoopy has a strong connection to the space program.

Snoopy, who had already taken on an important role as NASA's safety mascot in 1968, was further honored in 1969 when the astronauts of Apollo 10 nicknamed their lunar module *Snoopy* and their command module *Charlie Brown*. *Snoopy* (and *Charlie Brown*!) soared out of Earth's gravity on May 18, 1969, on their way to perform a "dress rehearsal" for the moon landing that was slated for July 1969. The astronauts of Apollo 10—Commander Thomas Stafford, Command Module Pilot John Young, and Lunar Module Pilot Eugene Cernan—carried paintings of Snoopy and Charlie Brown aboard their spacecraft and were also surprised to find original Schulz drawings of Snoopy, hidden by backup crew members, in their onboard checklists! Stafford and Cernan piloted *Snoopy* within fifty thousand feet of the lunar surface as they scouted the landing area for the Apollo 11 mission. After the linkup, *Snoopy* was jettisoned (and entered the sun's orbit where it remains to this day) and the crew started their long journey home. On May 26, 1969, command module *Charlie Brown* returned all three astronauts safely back to the Earth, concluding a very successful mission.

In the first of these photographs, Jamye Flowers (Coplin) waits in the hallway to spring a prank on Eugene Cernan, as Tom Stafford walks by and gives Snoopy a pat on the nose.

A close-up view of Charlie Brown and Snoopy riding the Mission Operations Control Room console at Mission Control Center in Houston, Texas, on the first day of the Apollo 10 mission, May 18, 1969.

NASA's Director of Flight Crew Operations Donald "Deke" Slayton and astronaut Charles Duke, Apollo 10's "CAPCOM" or capsule communicator, with Snoopy and Charlie Brown in the foreground at the Mission Control Center in Houston, Texas. The CAPCOM was generally another astronaut and the only person who communicated directly with the astronauts in space. It was believed that another astronaut, the CAPCOM, would be most able to understand the situation in the spacecraft and pass information along in the clearest and most efficient way.

Space and Space Travel

WHAT IS SPACE?

Space is the huge area beyond the Earth's atmosphere (the air that surrounds the Earth). You can't breathe in space because there is no air; astronauts have to take a supply of air with them. Space is very cold—nearly 460 degrees below zero Fahrenheit. BRRRR!

WHY DO WE NEED ROCKETS?

A rocket is a kind of motor or engine that is needed to lift a very heavy spacecraft off the Earth, break free from Earth's gravity, and fly through space. To pull away from Earth's gravity, a rocket must be traveling twenty-five thousand miles per hour!

WHO ARE THE ASTRONAUTS?

When the space program was first getting started, all of the astronauts were men. Many were engineers and pilots before they became astronauts. The first American woman astronaut was Dr. Sally Ride, a scientist and an athlete. She flew into space in 1983. Nowadays both men and women are astronauts. Maybe you will be an astronaut one day!

A funny fact: Astronauts on long space missions can grow an inch or two taller because there is no gravity in space and the bones in their spines move apart slightly. Once an astronaut returns to Earth—and to gravity—they shrink back to their normal size!

WHEN DO ASTRONAUTS NEED SPACE SUITS?

Space suits keep the astronauts safe and healthy whenever the astronaut leaves the spacecraft to take a space walk or walk on the moon as the Apollo astronauts did nearly fifty years ago. Some people think of space suits as a separate little spacecraft because they protect the astronauts from the extreme heat and cold of space and provide them with air to breathe.

Launch a Balloon Rocket

MATERIALS: balloon, paper clip, tape, straw, paper cup, string

INSTRUCTIONS:

1. Blow up a balloon and use a paper clip to hold the end closed.

2. Tape a straw to the balloon.

3. Add a paper cup to the end of the balloon as a nose.

4. Thread the string through the straw and stretch it tight.

5. Remove the paper clip and watch your rocket go.

The air rushing out of the balloon pushes against the air in the room. This is called *thrust*. Real rockets create thrust by burning fuel. Can you get your rocket to fly any faster or farther? Experiment to find out which type of balloon goes the farthest (round, long, etc.). Does the size of the straw affect how far the rocket travels? Does the nose help or hurt your flight? What else can you change to make your rocket fly farther?

Petaluma?

In this book, Charlie Brown encourages Snoopy to go to Petaluma, California, to compete in the annual World's Wrist Wrestling Championship. Snoopy sets off on his trek, using a globe as his map, eager to compete.

Believe it or not, this championship was real!

SKIP SOMMER
FOR THE *ARGUS-COURIER* |
August 28, 2016, 12:01 A.M.

In 1952, in a small saloon in Petaluma, *Argus-Courier* columnist Bill Soberanes witnessed a couple of guys wrist wrestling and thought it would be a pretty good draw for the community to sponsor a contest.

Soberanes never dreamed, however, what a big deal this would be and how "wrist wrestling" would become as synonymous with the name of Petaluma as chickens, when he saw Oliver Kolberg defeat Jack Homell at "Diamond Mike" Gilardi's corner saloon that day.

The contest was first called The Petaluma Wrist Wrestling Championship. But it shortly became the Northern California Championship, then went statewide and, in 1962, Bill teamed up with promoter Dave Devoto and formed The World Wrist Wrestling Championship.

Contestants came from all over the world, too. It was not unusual to have more than 300 guys (and gals) competing in 35 different divisions. The first World Unlimited Champion was Earl Hagerman.

By 1968, cartoonist Charles M. Schulz penned a series of 11 comic strips that sent Snoopy to Petaluma to compete in the WWC. Unfortunately, Schulz had the famous pup eliminated early on in his wrist-wrestling career, because it was noticed that he didn't have a thumb.

The *Peanuts* strips were distributed throughout the world and gave the WWC an even larger audience.

Peanuts is distributed internationally by Andrews McMeel Syndication.

Snoopy to the Rescue copyright © 2017 by Peanuts Worldwide, LLC. All rights reserved. Printed in China. No part of this book may be used or reproduced in any manner whatsoever without written permission except in the case of reprints in the context of reviews.

Andrews McMeel Publishing
a division of Andrews McMeel Universal
1130 Walnut Street, Kansas City, Missouri 64106

www.andrewsmcmeel.com

www.peanuts.com

20 21 22 23 24 SDB 10 9 8 7 6 5 4 3

ISBN: 978-1-4494-8206-0

Library of Congress Control Number: 2016950041

Made by:
King Yip (Dongguan) Printing & Packaging Factory Ltd.
Address and location of manufacturer:
Daning Administrative District, Humen Town
Dongguan Guangdong, China 523930
3rd Printing—7/27/20

ATTENTION: SCHOOLS AND BUSINESSES

Andrews McMeel books are available at quantity discounts with bulk purchase for educational, business, or sales promotional use. For information, please e-mail the Andrews McMeel Publishing Special Sales Department:
specialsales@amuniversal.com.

Check out more *Peanuts* kids' collections from Andrews McMeel Publishing.